Breakfast in the Barnyard

by JTK Belle

Illustrated by Mike Motz

Printed in the United States of America
First Printing, 2019

ISBN: 978-0-578-51354-6

JTK Belle is Jeff, Tommy, and Katie Belle.
Editor in Chief: Katie Belle
Creative Director: Tommy Belle
Illustrations by Mike Motz
Book Design by Michelle M White

Picklefish Press
Seatle, Washington
www.picklefishpress.com

Picklefish
Press

For Charlie Burwell

Hay for the horses,

corn for the cows,

grass for the sheep,

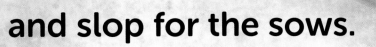

and slop for the sows.

Milk for the kittens,

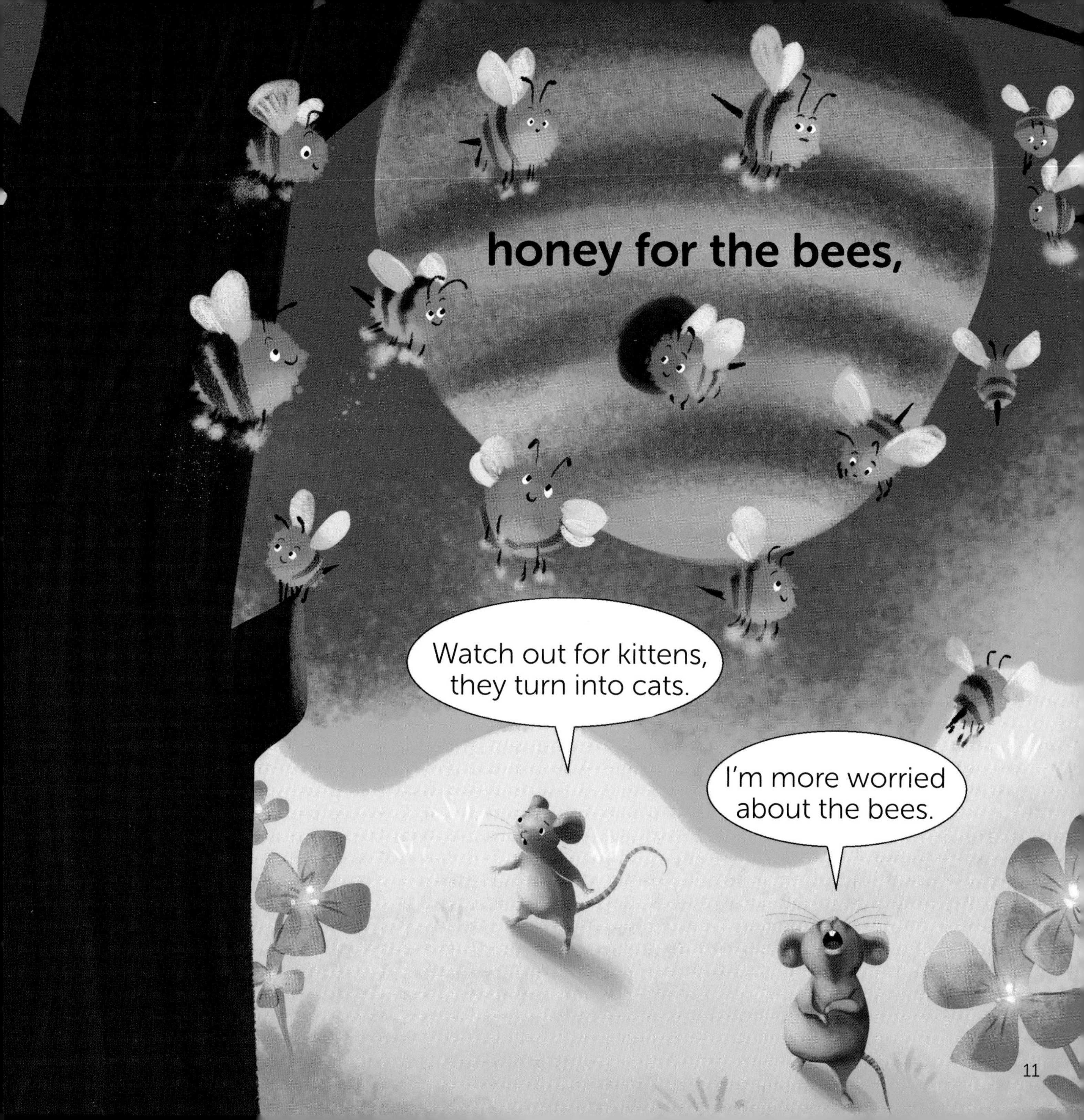

honey for the bees,

YUM-E-CHEESE

a worm for the bird,

and the mice eat cheese.

Wood for the woodchuck,

flies for the frog,

This cheese is stale.

It still tastes better than flies.

15

a nut for
the squirrel,

and a bone for the dog.

Where did they get this cheese?

From the trash can.

A carrot for the rabbit

and a grub for the mole,

an egg for the fox,
and he eats it
in his hole.

Rub-a-dub-dub...

Thanks for
the grub!

Leaves for the ladybug,

a fish for the duck,

which he catches by the tail.

The possum eats the grapes
that he picked from the vine.

Look what I found!

More CHEESE

Woo hoo!

It's bark from a tree for the porcupine.

The owl eats mice,

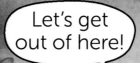

and the geese eat wheat,

and there's nothing at all
that the goat won't eat!

29

"Hay for the horses
Corn for the cows
Grass for the sheep
& slop for the sows!

Milk for the kittens
Honey for the bees
A worm for the bird
& the mice eat cheese!

Wood for the woodchuck
Flies for the frog
A nut for the squirrel
& a bone for the dog!

Carrots for the rabbit
And a grub for the mole
An egg for the fox
& he eats it in his hole!"

"Leaves for the ladybug
Lettuce for the snail
A fish for the duck
That he catches by the tail!

The possum eats the grapes
That he picked from the vine

It's bark from the tree
For the porcupine!

The owl eats mice
And the geese eat wheat
And there's nothing at all
That a goat won't eat!"

About the Authors

**JTK Belle is Jeff, Tommy, and Katie Belle.
They live in Seattle, Washington.**